Dugout Dreams

www.mascotbooks.com

Dugout Dreams

Cover illustration by Ann Leedy

For more information, please contact:
Mascot Books, an imprint of Amplify Publishing Group
620 Herndon Parkway, Suite 220
Herndon, VA 20170
info@mascotbooks.com
Library of Congress Control Number: 2023921924
CPSIA Code: PRV0324A
ISBN-13: 978-1-63755-964-2
Printed in the United States

To Kerri, for everything.

To Mom and Dad, for creativity and courage,
and baseball.

To Brooke and Jake, for keeping life interesting.

MATT LEEDY

Dugout Dreams

The Heart and Heartbreak of a
Travel Baseball Team

A Novella

MASCOT
B O O K S
an imprint of Amplify Publishing Group

FIRST INNING

STRIKE THREE.

A slight smile turns up the ends of Mark Balfoure's goatee, which a wad of tobacco in his left cheek has made a bit uneven. "Little prick," he says to no one. Balfoure puts down his cell phone and fishes out another Coors Light from the ice chest next to him. He stares for a moment at his meticulously groomed backyard and crystal-blue pool; his imagination overlays on the green grass a twelve-year-old dragging his bat back to the dugout, shoulders slumped, head down.

That kid doesn't belong anywhere near a baseball diamond, that much was obvious when he didn't have the spine to stick it out with me, Balfoure thinks. *If he had, he'd at least be on a winning team. Sure, he'd be watching us win from the bench, but that's a whole hell of a lot better than this: dragging his ass back to the dugout after striking out again in front of dozens—maybe even hundreds—of parents, other players, and coaches.*

Balfoure can't say for sure how many people witnessed the strikeout. The app he uses to follow the game doesn't have many details. From his backyard nearly three thousand miles away from the ball field, Balfoure can only make out the basics of the game: balls and strikes, outs, and base runners. He knows the strikeout victim well, coached him for years, and knows he belongs on the bench, not at the plate. More to the point, the boy's failure confirms Balfoure's thoughts: he should be the one coaching this game and leading a team of players handpicked to win the travel baseball Youth World Series in Cooperstown, New York.

A fresh beer in hand, Balfoure returns his gaze to his cell phone screen, glowing with dots and shapes. He imagines the other boys on the team who once played for him, good players, good boys, at least before they and their parents turned against him. In his head, he can hear the hollers that are surely filling the Cooperstown air: "That's alright. That's OK. Let's hold 'em now. Three up. Three down." Humph. He grins again, using the break between innings to scan through the images saved on his phone. Switching to Facebook, where some of the parents who are sitting in the Cooperstown stands are still his "friends," he posts a quote from legendary Alabama football coach Nick Saban:

"Bouncing from team to team because you don't get your way is a habit that has been taught and accepted in the youth sports culture."

SECOND INNING

COACH BALFOURE TAKES HIS SEAT on a bucket just outside the visitors' dugout as his team of twelve-year-olds jogs onto the field. Switching a plug of Copenhagen from one cheek to another, he thinks to himself, *Not the best team, but they'll do*.

In the aluminum bleachers, moms scan the field for their sons. The women are a team of their own, decked in matching navy tank tops with the word "Sluggers" scrawled across their chests in red cursive. "That's My Boy" is emblazoned on their backs above large numbers that match their sons' uniforms. Every letter, every number bedazzled.

"Tell me again who we're playing," Jaclyn asks.

The moms sigh. It's on the schedule and the tournament bracket that Coach Balfoure texted to everyone last night. The moms exchange glances and without words agree, at least this time she got Jason to the field in the right uniform.

"Seriously, who are we playing?" Jaclyn asks.

"SBA," the other ladies answer in chorus. "Santiago Baseball Academy."

Dads stride to the field from their white pickup trucks, their round stomachs filled with Coors Light. They split into clusters, some behind the backstop, some down the right-field line, others next to their wives in the stands. Their cheeks bulge with sunflower seeds.

Tapping his nose, his right cheek, and his nose again, Coach Balfoure relays a signal to his catcher. It's a language he and his son, Rick, know well. From his squat behind the plate, Rick points a single finger toward the dirt. Fastball.

"God damn it, he's got Alex playing right field," Craig grouses to himself and to the other dads within earshot. He leans against a chain-link fence that borders the right-field foul line, empties his right cheek of sunflower seeds, and replaces them with loose-leaf tobacco. "He knows Alex belongs at second. That's where he'll be in high school. He needs to get comfortable in the infield."

"At least your boy is in," Seth says, nodding to the Sluggers' dugout where Zach is peeling the label from his energy drink.

In the third inning, Alex creeps from the on-deck

circle to the batter's box for the first time this morning. Craig strides from his perch on the chain-link fence to an open spot behind the backstop. "Swing it! Swing it hard!"

Alex looks at his father but is otherwise motionless. Strike one. Then another.

Craig's eyes bulge. "Get the bat off your shoulder! Jesus Christ! Swing it!"

A pitch snaps into the catcher's glove just as Alex lifts his bat from his back shoulder. Strike three.

Craig throws up his hands and marches toward the parking lot. On the way, he passes his youngest son, Austin. The nine-year-old is occupied in his own world of construction make-believe, pushing Matchbox trucks through a patch of dirt and weeds.

"Unbelievable."

Despite a litany of errors and strikeouts, the Sluggers eke out a two-to-one win.

"You boys were lucky," Coach Balfoure tells his players, who kneel in a semicircle around him. "Two runs? That's not going to cut it. I don't care if you strike out, but swing the god damn bat for Christ's sake."

After his opening salvo, Balfoure continues his tirade for another twenty minutes, recapping each of the seven innings, all the errors and every strikeout. Parents with folding chairs slung over their shoulders creep closer to the semicircle, trying to stay in Balfoure's sight line. Craig is at his pickup, downing Coors Lights until the Sluggers are finally released back to the dugout to gather their bats and gloves.

Alex doesn't bother to look for his father. Instead, he finds Austin in the dirt and weeds. "Let's go," Alex tells his little brother. "Game's over."

Anxiety mounts inside Alex with the knowledge that his dad is waiting, waiting with critiques of every at-bat, every ground ball, every inning. He scoops up the toy trucks and grabs his little brother by the arm, brushes the dirt from his knees.

"Come on, let's go. Dad's waiting."

The Sluggers' narrow victory brings no joy to Zach either. Aside from pinch running and an uneventful moment on the basepaths, he spent the entire afternoon on the bench.

Zach watches the baseball players, parents, and umpires walk to their cars as his dad steers their pickup truck out of the parking lot. Nothing interests him on the other side of his passenger window; he stares blankly at the tract homes, community mailboxes, telephone poles. Soon they're on the highway, and Zach is relieved. They've made it this long in silence, and now there's a good chance the silence will continue uninterrupted until they reach home. There will be no talk of the game, of why he didn't play, or barely played, or of all the possible reasons why. Zach leans his head against the window.

Two-acre ranches pass by with solitary white-brown horses and white-black cows, hemmed in by sagging barbed-wire fences. Soon there are bright, white fences. Then broken-down, rotting fences. Then fences with posts adorned with horseshoes painted in alternating red, white, and blue paint. They pass by a flag with the words "Let's Go Brandon." Zach imagines that Brandon must be a varsity high school baseball player with parents who have plenty of reasons to cheer during every game.

The road unfurls impossibly long before them. Zach painstakingly counts down the number of telephone poles before he knows they'll be home, and he can retreat to his bedroom where the frenetic energy of Fortnite will blot out memories of the game.

Seth considers the pointlessness of the ride as well. "God damn it. We're up at the crack of dawn for what? A full tank of gas, a Saturday afternoon, for what?"

Finally home, Zach drops his bat bag in the garage and hurries through the kitchen, then the living room, and turns down the hallway to his room. He winces when his father's voice reverberates through the kitchen, the living room, and his bedroom walls. "Don't put your pants in the laundry. Just leave them. They can't possibly be dirty. That goes for the rest of your uniform, too." Without waiting for a response, "Did you hear me, Zach?"

"Seth, what's wrong? What happened?" Monica asks her husband.

Seth stares in the direction of Zach's room. "It's going to be an early morning again tomorrow. It's an eight o'clock game. I guarantee coach is going to want us there by seven. Damn it, just once could we manage a win on Saturday and not have to wake up at the crack of dawn on Sunday?"

"Was it bad? What happened with Zach?"

"We'll need to leave by six fifteen, at the latest."

"You still haven't told me what happened. How'd he do? Did we win?"

"We won, but all he did was pinch run. And you know what? I'm tired of waking up early every weekend and sitting for two hours just to watch him pinch run."

"Well, what do you think we should do? Can you talk to coach?"

"Fine."

"I mean it's not fair to Zach. And he's not having any fun. Christ, Seth, he's in his room probably hating this more than you."

"I said fine, I'll call him, OK. What else do you want me to do?"

"Seth, I wish you would just calm down. I'm just saying," Monica sighs, fatigued from the day's errands. "Now what do you want to do about dinner? Ribs, maybe?"

"We don't have time for ribs, Monica. I'll do those burgers that have been sitting in the freezer forever. If the boys keep playing like they have been, we'll be home tomorrow in plenty of time for ribs."

In his room, Zach pulls off his uniform, flips on his PlayStation, and places a headset over his ears. Rapid-fire bullet sprays spitting from Fortnite combatants mask the noise from the next room. Zach sees Alex's avatar appear on the screen, and soon his friend is in his ear.

"Well, at least I didn't strike out," Zach says.

"Whatever, at least I got an at-bat," Alex says before hunting down virtual opponents quickly consumes their attention.

Seth slaps hamburger patties onto the grill and pulls his cell phone from a pocket in his cargo shorts.

He stares at the phone and slowly taps out a phone number.

"Hey Coach, how's it going? Tough one today, huh? . . . Listen, you're doing a great job with the boys. Their bats will heat up. Law of averages, right? . . ."

Balfoure takes the phone from his ear and looks at the screen in frustration first and then sighs. He knows what Seth is ramping up to. The first post-game phone call of the day from a dad upset about his son's playing time. He's heard it many times before: "Tough one today." "You're doing a great job." "Their bats will heat up." Balfoure knows what Seth's backhanded encouragement means: put my mediocre son in the game even if he shouldn't be on the team to begin with. *Well, fuck off, Seth*, he thinks and loudly talks over the transparent pleasantries.

"Seth, they've got to swing the god damn bat and start taking it seriously. This isn't little league. This isn't all-stars. Travel ball isn't a cake walk. The boys have got to earn it. We had tryouts for a reason."

"About that," Seth says. "Zach didn't even have a chance to swing it today. Like I said, I think you're doing a great job. But Zach hit nearly .400 during the regular season this year. I'm not saying he'll do the same in travel, but you know . . . We love playing for the Sluggers.

We always have. But 250 bucks a month, plus uniforms and gas money, and soon it will be hotels. I mean . . ."

"Fine," Balfoure says. "I'll see you tomorrow."

Seth thumbs through a stack of bills. He orders them into three piles. The first to be mailed Monday, must be mailed Monday. Half of the second pile hopefully can be paid next week, barring anything unexpected. The third, umph, pointless even opening those envelopes.

He breathes deeply and then writes a check for $250, made out to "Sluggers, c/o Mark Balfoure."

THIRD INNING

Ball four.

On the mound, Jason pounds his right fist into his glove and snaps his mitt at the ball when it's thrown back. As base runners circle around him like a slow-motion carousel, he peers at the dirt mound, searching for answers. He wonders if he's bending his back and finishing his pitches. Is he over striding? Under striding? He looks to his coach.

"Don't look at me. Figure it out," Coach Balfoure yells. "And figure it out quick. Like now!"

In the aluminum bleachers, another father, Jackson, loudly asks, "What's it going to take to get another pitcher in there?" He rises from his place in the stands and joins the dads lined up against a waist-high fence bordering the left-field foul line. His son, Jackson Jr., or J.J., is at third base and has begun to lose interest. "J.J. get in the game. Cover your bag when he gets a lead like that. Picking him off might be the only way we get an out this inning."

Jason ignores the slight and slides his foot against the rubber. *Reach for the plate*, he thinks. *Finish the pitch. Dear God, just don't walk another batter.*

Ball one, ball two, ball three, ball four.

Jason doesn't bother to look at his coach. He takes the ball from his catcher in disgust and walks slowly back to the mound. *What is wrong with me today?* Jason peers at his catcher's fingers to get the next sign. Like it matters at this point. He has no idea where it's going. Everybody can see that. *Screw it.*

Ping!

Zach turns his hips and races full stride as the ball soars toward deep right field. He takes a diagonal path to the foul line, then turns his hips once more and veers toward center field. He looks up and his head cocks, shifting from his right shoulder to his left, then back again. He reaches up and feels the ball smack the palm of his glove.

Good call putting Zach in right field instead of Alex, Coach Balfoure thinks as he rises from his bucket. A base runner from third barely has time to cross the plate on the sacrifice fly before Balfoure takes his first step onto the infield. He extends his right hand, and Jason meekly hands him the ball.

"I wanted you to get at least one out before I pulled you," Balfoure says. "Take center field. Bring Phil in here. And while you're out there, maybe thank Zach for saving your ass. That looked like a home run off the bat."

Jason throws his glove against the dugout fence, snatches it back up, and throws it to the ground. His dad covers half his face with his right hand. Patrick then pulls his cell phone from his sweatpants and sighs deeply, thinking about how to describe the past forty-five minutes of struggle to Jason's private pitching coach.

"I don't know what's going on with him today, but I have video. I'll send it. You tell me what you see," Patrick says. "How about we do an extra session next week? Maybe tweak a few things. Let me know what works for you."

Zach slouches against the chain-link dugout and feels a tug on his jersey. "Hey buddy. Hey, look at me," Seth says. "Great catch out there. Defense is important but listen up. Are you listening? You guys are down four runs. This game might be over, but make sure you get your cuts in. Go ahead, grip it and rip it."

Zach hustles to grab his batting helmet, batting gloves, and bat. Soon the new pitcher's warm-up throws are over, and it's time. Zach digs his cleats into the batter's box. Seth yells, "Swing hard, Zach. Swing hard in case you hit it." Parents laugh, and Seth smiles. *Seriously though*, he thinks to himself, *swing the bat*.

Zach jumps on a waist-high fastball and laces it into the gap between left and center field. The ball bounces hard against the fence, and Zach jogs into second base, claps his hands, and points to his teammates. "Let's go!"

"Yes! Yes! I told you," Seth says, pumping a fist. "He jumped on that meatball."

Zach's heroics produce the Sluggers' only highlights. After losing to the Rockets five to one, they're eliminated from the "Dust Up in Dry Creek" tournament.

During the procession to the parking lot, Patrick tries to keep pace with Balfoure's quick strides. "Hey, Coach. Coach! Hey. I don't know what was up with Jason today, but he'll get right."

"Don't worry about it. I'll see you at practice," Balfoure says, turning his attention to his old friend making his way to the field, a former junior college teammate and current coach of the Rockets. "Hey, what's up, Greg? Good luck out there. We shit the bed, but hopefully you do better in the championship. Call me after."

"Thanks Mark, will do. You've got some good little ballplayers this year. Today was just our day. Better to be lucky than good. Anyway, maybe we can get together during the week and scrimmage sometime. And I'll let you know how it goes in the championship."

God damn it, Balfoure thinks, *if he had Greg's line-up, he wouldn't need any luck.* He spits a stream of tobacco juice and notices Patrick has been lingering a few paces away, eager to finish a conversation about Jason's struggles on the mound. Balfoure doesn't have the time or patience to listen to another dad's explanation of his son's failure.

Heartache is part of the game that Balfoure has endured. He played well in high school, but not well enough to attract the college scholarship offers he coveted. And he played well in junior college, better even than his friend and teammate Greg, he remembers. But it was Greg who went on to play Division I college baseball on a partial scholarship, while Balfoure's playing days ended. He turned to selling insurance, then mortgage loans, and, once he finally passed his real estate license exam, homes. Baseball became something he could only watch wistfully on television when he wasn't walking clients through one house after another.

His son's birth reignited hope. Balfoure coached Rick's little league team, and when his son turned seven, he volunteered (in earnest) to coach the league's youngest all-star team. It wasn't long before Balfoure decided the league's stars didn't shine bright enough to match Rick's burgeoning talent.

Balfoure filed the necessary paperwork to form a nonprofit travel team, allowing him to draw players from throughout the city—and beyond—regardless of the geographical boundaries of local little leagues. Balfoure's travel team, the Sluggers, would provide Rick with the opportunity to play with, and against, similarly skilled ball players. The weekend travel tournaments would prepare his son for a high school career that would draw the attention of college scouts. Scholarship offers would follow. After that, who knows?

Catering to insecure parents, anxious about their sons' play, was never part of the plan.

He starts making his way to his truck. "Drive safe," Balfoure tells Patrick, who stands silently in the parking lot with Jason by his side.

Seth is also eager to flee the long faces on the Sluggers and the other parents. "Great game Zach, great game," he says as he clicks on the air conditioning and calls home, placing his cell phone on speaker. "Hey babe. Yeah, you should have been here. I have good news and more good news. Zach played great. Had a great catch and hammered a double."

"Oh, that's great," Monica's voice drifts out from the

phone. "So, what's your plan?"

"We're on our way home. Oh, yeah, we lost. Five to one, six to one, I'm not sure," Seth says. "But anyway, we lost, we're knocked out of the tourney. Whatever. Plenty of time for ribs tonight."

FOURTH INNING

ALEX LEANS AGAINST THE CINDER BLOCK wall that divides the classroom wings of his middle school and the basketball courts. The concrete is hot against his back, and the asphalt beneath is just as uncomfortable. *Thank God there's only a couple weeks of school left.* He stares ahead, past the boys shooting hoops, to the girls on the other side of the courts, huddled together, talking and giggling.

"Take a picture, weirdo." It's Brianna. Surrounded by friends, she stands out and not just because she's half a foot taller than everyone else. Her wavy brown hair reaches her waist, and she appears just a year or two younger than the babysitters who watch over her peers.

Alex looks down at his Nikes. *Shit.* He wasn't even looking at her. *God, I can't wait for school to be over.*

Zach notices. So does Jason. Just about all the boys notice just about everything Brianna says and does.

Zach steps out of the line for free throws and tugs on Jason's shirt.

"Hey, Jason, check it out," Zach says. "Come on."

"What? I'm next. Hang on."

"No seriously, Jason, come on," Zach says, pulling him by the arm from the shooting contest toward the cinder block wall.

Alex stands, crumples an empty chip bag in his hands, and nods at the boys. "Hey, what's up?"

"Nothing man, why don't you come shoot some hoops?" Zach says.

"Nah, too hot," Alex says. "Besides lunch is almost over anyway. Isn't it?"

"Yeah, I guess," Zach says as he sits down against the wall. "Basketball is boring anyway. Hey, you guys going to practice tonight? Coach is going to run us hard. Damn, I hate losing, but I hate running more. He's going to be pissed."

"Yeah, he is," Jason says. "He's going to run *my* ass for sure. Not that it's going to help me find the strike zone. Damn."

"He's going to run all of us," Zach says. "Run me too. Even though I had that double and kept you from giving up even more runs. Not sure you would have ever gotten out of that inning if I hadn't run down that fly ball."

"You got lucky," Jason says. "You looked drunker than my dad trying to run that thing down. Luck, pure luck. Besides, I didn't even get out of the inning, I got pulled."

"I shouldn't have to run at all," Alex says. "Didn't even get into that game."

The bell rings, and the boys slowly get to their feet.

"Well, hopefully coach is in a good mood tonight," Zach says. "Come on, let's go. And Alex, screw Brianna. She thinks she's the shit now but wait till high school. There's going to be way hotter girls. All over the place."

"Let's go, boys. If you don't have your cleats on don't worry. You're going to need your running shoes tonight," Coach Balfoure shouts. "You know the drill. Foul pole to foul pole. Hurry it up."

The Sluggers line up as Balfoure places his whistle between his lips and blows. The boys lurch ahead and ease into a jog. Balfoure blows the whistle again. "Back in line. Back in line! This isn't a walk through the park. These are burners. You boys owe me from last weekend. If you're not going to hit, you're going to run. Now let's go."

The sun begins to melt away above the left-field foul line, and the Sluggers' legs have long since faded. "Alright boys, that's it," Balfoure shouts. "Break down the field. Jason, Alex, you're coming with me and Rick. I'm taking you home tonight."

The boys toss their equipment into the pickup bed and climb into the cab. Before they're out of the parking lot, Balfoure starts in on his favorite topic. "You know we're going to have a separate tryout for the team we take to Cooperstown, right?"

Jason and Alex stare blankly out the window, wondering whether mac and cheese or pizza is waiting for them at home.

"I had to buy that Cooperstown bid, and it wasn't cheap," Balfoure continues. "Those teams out there are going to be good. Better than what we faced last weekend. And nobody wants to go all the way across the country just to get our asses handed to us. But it's going to be awesome. The fields are perfect. You'll stay in dorms, play morning, noon, and night." Balfoure leans forward, excited now, he rolls down the driver's side window and spits a stream of tobacco juice. "I'm getting ready to order the pins. Every team comes with pins, and at lunch and dinner and between games, you guys trade them with other teams. And Jeter is getting into the Hall of Fame that weekend, so the place is going to be packed. Bunch of folks go to the games, too. You won't just be playing in front of your parents."

Balfoure looks back at the boys nodding off behind him.

"It's not cheap though, which is why you boys have to prove yourselves. Nobody wants to pay all that money just to watch you lose."

Alex opens his door before Balfoure comes to a stop.

"Whoa, just a sec," Balfoure says, pressing down hard on the brakes. "You afraid you're going to be late for dinner?"

Alex pulls his baseball bag from the back of the pickup bed, no longer caring if it's going to be mac and cheese or pizza.

"Greg, how the hell are you?" Balfoure says as he greets his former teammate at home plate. "I'd ask you to take it easy on us today, but I know better."

"Shit, it's not like we've been setting the world on fire," Greg says. "We got shut out last week in the championship game. You never know what you're going to get from these little fuckers."

Umpire Harry Boyd interrupts.

"All right gentlemen, it's just about that time. Now there's nothing I can tell you that you don't already know. Just do me a favor and try to keep your parents under control. I didn't come out here to eat shit all day while I sweat my balls off."

Harry's black, oversized shirt is stretched tight across his massive frame. The bulge from his midsection presses hard against his chest protector. His feet strain the sides of his black, worn sneakers, stained a grimy yellowish-white from flour and oil, remnants of his job managing a local pizzeria.

In his right hand, he fumbles with a home plate brush. His right index finger, the one umpires use to call strikes, is missing down to the middle knuckle, having been crushed in a long-ago car crash.

"I'm serious," Harry continues. "If it's the same bull-shit as last tournament, I won't hesitate to throw either one of you out. I'll toss you, the drunk-ass dad, and Mommy Dearest, and you can all take a walk together to the parking lot. Shit's getting old."

"Jesus Christ, Knuckle, take it easy," Balfoure says. "Try to make your fuckups somewhat equitable, and we'll keep it to a minimum."

Harry takes a swig from his water bottle, crams

it into the chain-link fence of the backstop and tells the Sluggers' catcher, Rick, "Two more warm-ups, then throw it down. We're already running behind."

Balfoure takes his seat on a bucket in the dugout entry. "This is going to be ugly."

But optimism radiates from the Sluggers' mothers.

"OK Jason, here we go. Rock and fire baby! Rock and fire!" Jaclyn says to her boy after he takes the last of his warm-up throws.

Thirty minutes later, the first inning mercifully comes to an end for the Sluggers. The damage: Four runs, three hits, two walks, one hit by pitch, and several errors.

"That's alright baby, we'll get 'em back," Jaclyn says, her voice trailing off. "Monica, take a lap with me?"

The women navigate the toddlers, mothers, blankets, nachos, and water jugs as they carefully step down the aluminum bleachers.

"Poor guy, that was the last thing he needed. It sure seems like our defense just goes to pot when he's pitching. I don't know, I just hope he doesn't get discouraged," Jaclyn says. "Hopefully, we score some runs. Who knows? I mean look at those boys on the Rockets. They're huge. They look more like men than twelve-year-olds."

"Jaclyn, hey," Monica says, her voice cracking.

"I'm sorry, dear, I just get so worked up when Jason is on the mound. You know how it is," Jaclyn says. "Your boy's been looking great lately. Zach's been getting a lot more playing time. He's looked good out there."

"Yeah, Jaclyn. Listen, I have to tell you something," Monica says. "I'm going to need help getting Zach to practice."

"Of course, girl, I don't see why we haven't organized a carpool by now anyway."

"There's something else," Monica says. Her voice catches. "Oh my god, I'm just going to say it: I have cancer. Breast cancer. I start chemo next week. They say it's stage one. They caught it early."

"Oh my god, Monica. Come here. What else did they say?"

Monica begins to cry. They hug, and, after a moment, Monica musters an answer.

"That's about it. Well, they're optimistic," she pauses. "Maybe that's the wrong word, I don't know. But it's stage one, and it's not near my lymph nodes. Anyway, I haven't told anyone else on the team yet. Maybe next week, but keep it between us for now."

"Have you and Seth said anything to Zach?"

"Not yet, I'm thinking Monday."

"OK, oh girl, I'm so sorry. But it's just stage one, right? That's good."

"Yeah, it is. It's just scary. I don't want to go through chemo, Jaclyn. Oh my god. I don't know. Thanks again for helping with Zach. Seth is going with me to the treatments, of course."

"Of course, girl, no problem. Zach can stay for dinner. Might be good for him to just hang out with a friend for a while."

"Well, we appreciate it. Let's head back. I don't want the moms to think we're gossiping."

On the field, the Sluggers aren't exactly slugging. Or fielding. The Rockets are flirting with the 10-run rule when Alex makes his first appearance.

And promptly strikes out.

Balfoure's post-game speech is brief for a change, and Alex's dad quickly intercepts his son.

"Don't beat yourself up, kid," Craig says. "Come on, get your stuff."

Alex methodically packs up his two bats, batting gloves, wrist bands, helmet, cleats, and elbow guard. He says nothing for fear that speaking might lead to tears. He wishes his dad, for once, would be quiet as well.

"The whole team sucked it up today," Craig says. "Hey, no reason to pout. I don't know what you expect when you only see three pitches the entire game. Hang on a sec, I'm going to have a word with coach."

"Please, Dad. Can we just go home?"

"Hey, Coach! Do you have a minute?"

Balfoure is already in a conversation with Greg when Craig sidles up to the coaches.

"Coach, do you have a sec?"

"Let's talk before practice, OK?" Balfoure says. "Or I can give you a call this evening, OK? How's Alex? We just need him to start swinging a little earlier. Like before the ball is in the catcher's mitt."

Craig winces. "Well, I think, I think he might just need a little encouragement."

Balfoure turns just enough to make eye contact. "We'll get him right. Try to build up his confidence in batting practice."

Craig walks away at the dismissal, and Balfoure quickly turns his back again, retraining his attention on Greg.

"You see what I have to deal with?" Balfoure says. "Now I'm going to have to spend two hours hearing about how his kid is the next Ken Griffey Jr. I mean, seriously? You saw him out there. Shit, he should be thanking me for just having his kid on the team, much less playing him at all. Anyway, whatever, I'll deal with that later. Listen, your boys looked good today. Like an actual baseball team. You decided yet if you're going to Cooperstown this year?"

"No, I doubt it. For one, I didn't put in for a bid. Our fundraising has been shit this year, and I don't know if we could even afford it," Greg says. "You're not the only one with problems. Half my kids are playing with another team. Some of my best guys. A bunch of them just turned twelve, and they're playing with a U13 team. I wouldn't be surprised if I lose them. They don't show up to practice. I'm lucky to get them to games. I was missing two today. Otherwise, we would have 10-run ruled your ass for sure."

"I'm surprised you didn't," Balfoure says. "But we've got some decent kids. You know my boy can hit."

"I know, I'm just giving you a hard time," Greg says. "You've got a few ballplayers. I'm not saying you don't."

"You know I got a bid, right? I'll have the fireworks stand going again this year. Along with a few other things—a couple raffles, some sponsorships I already have locked up—I'll have most of the expenses covered. Cooperstown is great, man. And we'll be there for Jeter's induction. If you really are going to lose those kids, and you want to go to Cooperstown, we should combine teams. Maybe play in some better tournaments where we don't have to chalk the foul lines and put up the fence ourselves. There's a good tourney coming up in Vegas. Think about it."

Alex pulls off his cleats, dumps his bat bag in the garage, and walks head down through the kitchen and to his bedroom. He jerks the protective cup from his sliding shorts and tosses it, and his hat, onto the floor.

Jennifer eyes her husband, trying to measure his anger, as he grabs a Coors Light from the refrigerator.

"Well, that must have been a fun ride home," she says. "What's up with Alex? Did you guys lose?"

"Lose? We got blown out. Eight, maybe nine to one; fuck, I don't know. I stopped counting," Craig says before swallowing several gulps of beer. "We were getting killed outta the gates; never stood a chance. And fucking Coach Balfoure. Fucking Balfoure didn't put Alex in until the last inning and then just to pinch hit. Just in time to make the last out. That motherfucker."

"Craig, calm down. Why didn't Alex get to play? He barely played last game. That's ridiculous. I mean, what's going on? Are you going to talk to Coach?"

"I tried. I tried after the game. The guy wouldn't

even look me in the eye. Completely blew me off."

"Did Alex say anything on the ride home?" Jennifer says. "I can tell he's upset. Was he crying?"

"No, he wasn't crying. He wasn't crying. Didn't say a word," Craig says, cracking a second beer. "Unbelievable. Un-fucking-believable."

"You have to calm down Craig. Why don't you watch the game? I turned it on for you. Looks like the Dodgers are winning at least. Let's just give Alex some space. I'll try to talk to him later."

Craig settles into his recliner and watches the Dodgers finish off the Diamondbacks. As commercials transition to postgame interviews, he drifts into sleep, a half-full Coors Light between his legs.

Jennifer eases Alex's bedroom door open and sees him curled in bed facing a wall that is floor-to-ceiling Los Angeles Dodgers: posters of Dodger Stadium, Clayton Kershaw, Cody Bellinger, and Corey Seager.

"Alex, baby, I know you're upset," Jennifer says, sitting next to her son, leaning in to stroke his matted brown hair. He recoils. "Listen, your dad and I are really proud of you. I know it wasn't easy to make the Sluggers. It's a real honor just to be picked. Think of all the boys that didn't make the cut. Do you remember how many boys showed up to that tryout?"

Alex squirms his body closer to the wall. His mother can feel his shoulders and back tremble. Jennifer looks up at Dodger Stadium and at all of Alex's heroes, remembering the day they put the posters up together.

Jennifer sighs. "Sweetheart, you know if you want to play on another team or try another sport, that's OK. Your dad and I will understand. I might do the same thing if I were you. We just want you to be happy."

"Just leave me alone, Mom."

"Alex, it's not the end of the world. I know you think it is, but it's not."

"Just go!"

"OK, I'll leave you alone, but please change out of that uniform before you come to dinner."

Alex shrugs. After his mom closes the bedroom door, all the words he wishes he could say to someone rush through his head.

Try another sport? Baseball is my sport because nothing else has ever been my sport. At first, I couldn't hide on a football field. I was small, but I couldn't hide. When the football found my hands or was placed in my gut, they found me. They were violent; they found me; they joyfully carried out skull-ringing tackles. I was a ball carrier they could launch five yards out of bounds with a clean hit from their shoulder pads. Their tackles brought cheers from one sideline and groans from the other. Until eventually, my coaches gave me a place I could hide. Assigned to the sidelines, with no chance of being launched, I could hide. Invisible. To coaches, to teammates, to everyone except my dad. My safe place was his disgust, and that was the end of football.

No one tackles you in basketball. When someone gets too close, pass the ball and action moves in another direction. Eyes are focused on the boys too big for their age. They shoot the shots and score the points. Pass and hide. Pass and hide. A season passes by without any shot attempts of my own. And my dad says that's the end of basketball.

Whatever. PlayStation and pajamas suit me just fine. But while my games load, I can hear my parents: "He's not making friends. He doesn't talk. He doesn't even make eye contact most of the time. He needs something."

"KING'S HARDWARE" had been stitched across the chest of my baseball uniform, and the maroon hat with a yellow "KH" never quite fit right, but it didn't matter. Alone on the pitcher's mound, I threw the ball past kids I knew from school. I could catch well enough. And even though my legs flailed outward when I ran, and I always felt like I was seconds from falling forward, *my awkward stride didn't draw attention. Every once in a while, I hit the ball with the barrel of my bat. I made friends without trying. They sat next to me in the dugout, and I was invited to birthday parties and swim parties. After games, my dad put his arm around me on the way to the parking lot. Practices were easy and fun. I joked, and my new friends laughed. We all laughed, no matter the score or our record, because no one seemed to care. After the season, my dad said I could try out for something called a "travel team." I nodded yes. Because baseball is my sport.*

But maybe I was wrong.

Hours later, Jennifer arranges forks, knives, and glasses for dinner. She places plates full of Alex's favorite chicken parmigiana on the dining room table. She walks to her son's room where she finds his Sluggers' uniform in a pile outside his bedroom door. Jennifer gathers the clothes and returns to the dining room where Craig is already cutting into his chicken.

"I found these outside his bedroom," Jennifer says. "I think you need to call coach and tell him Alex is quitting."

"I'll talk to him in the morning. Let him sleep on it," Craig says. "And if he wants to quit, he should have to man up and do it himself."

"Craig, listen to yourself. He's not a man. He's twelve."

"Fine, but if I have to do it, I want to look Balfoure in the eye."

FIFTH INNING

JACLYN IS UP EARLY, two hours before the Sluggers' eight o'clock game. Cracking egg after egg, scrambling, adding bacon and cheese, and wrapping it all in tortillas. She doesn't notice when Patrick, who is mildly impressed with this one-woman assembly line, enters the kitchen.

"So, the fundraising begins. How many breakfast burritos is it going to take to buy one of those cool caps?"

"First of all, they're called cold caps. And we're not just selling burritos, we have permission from the park to sell candy and soda. I've got boxes of the stuff from Costco yesterday. I just left them in the trunk. And Jennifer had those 'Strike Out Cancer' tank tops made up that we'll sell at the tournament. They cost us $15 each, and we're selling them for $20. We don't even know how much the cold cap treatment costs. We decided to pitch in so the expense won't keep her from trying the treatment if that's what she wants. I know she's worried about losing her hair, and the cold caps are supposed to help."

Patrick nods, wishing he hadn't asked, having forgotten what he did ask, and far more interested in the last step in his wife's burrito endeavor.

"Whoa, whoa, whoa. You're using my ice chest?"

"Yes, Patrick, it's the only thing we have that will keep them warm. You can go a game or two without beer. The tournament has two morning games today at eight and ten for Christ's sake. Do you boys really think you're fooling anyone, standing around in the parking lot before games, between games, after games . . ." Jaclyn continues, not noticing he's left the kitchen.

Patrick drops Jason off at the ballpark an hour before game time and heads back to his truck. Plenty of time. He drives three blocks to a Johnny Quick for a pint of Jim Beam. Patrick leaves a ten dollar bill on the counter, grabs the booze in a brown paper bag, and leaves without waiting for the cashier to give him his change. Soon he's back in the parking lot beyond left field.

Patrick pulls up alongside Seth, hops down from his truck, and motions for his friend to join him. Patrick takes a sip and passes the bottle.

Seth smiles. "Nice. Straight for the hard stuff. Why haven't we thought of this before?"

"Special occasion," Patrick says. "Jaclyn has my ice chest loaded up with burritos. You know the fundraiser thing the ladies have going for those, what are they called, cold caps? Speaking of which, how is Monica feeling?"

"She feels fine for now. No different really. Not yet," Seth says, taking another sip. "She doesn't start chemo for another week. Hopefully that chemo just knocks this thing out. Her doctor thinks it will. But he also says the treatments will make things worse before it gets better. Long road ahead . . . I'm worried about Zach; about how he's going to handle seeing his mom sick. It's all scary, for Monica, for me, but I'm afraid it's going to be even worse for Zach."

"He's got his friends. He's got you, and he's got Monica. And Monica, she's tough," Patrick says. "And we'll be there for all of you. You know that. Monica will beat this. And I'm sure Zach will be fine."

Seth passes the bottle back. "I'm not so sure."

Patrick stares at the black asphalt, takes a swig. Uncomfortable in the silence, he retreats to their shared language of travel baseball. "I heard from Craig that Alex is quitting. Today will be his last game with us.

Craig texted me last night, plans to tell Balfoure before the game. Craig should be here any minute."

"No shit? He didn't tell me, but I could tell he was steamed after the last game. Probably best he does it with a crowd. Less likely to turn into a fight," Seth says.

"Agreed. There he is now. Let's walk with him," Patrick says, handing Seth the bottle. "Here, put this in your jacket. I kinda told Jaclyn I wouldn't drink this tournament."

Craig strides purposefully across the parking lot. He reassures himself, *My son isn't a quitter, we're not quitters, but Alex can't play on this team any longer. It's no good for him. And Balfoure needs to hear it and look me in the eyes when I say it, that we've had enough. That Alex has had enough.*

"Hey Craig, come here! Craig, hey, come here for a second," Seth says, breaking Craig from his trance and motioning him to the spot between pickup trucks where Seth and Patrick are waiting for the pregame warm-ups to wrap up.

Seth's voice lifts the angry fog from Craig's thoughts, and he walks to his friends. "Seth, Patrick, how are you? Boys, I've been struggling with this, but I don't think this is the right team for Alex anymore. We're done."

"I know, and I don't think you're wrong," Patrick

says. "But this team isn't the end-all, be-all of baseball. You've got to do what's right for your boy . . . Hang out for a bit. Seth, give him a swig. Just chill out. Hang out with us for one more game."

Craig accepts the bottle from Seth and takes a long pull. "I appreciate it. I've got nowhere to be, but I've got to talk to Coach Balfoure first. Tell him about Alex. Take care of this and then I can hang out. I can't leave anyway, even if I wanted to, Jennifer has all these shirts she's made up to help Monica."

Craig takes another drink. "Alright, let me handle this, and I'll find you."

The Sluggers finish the last of their warm-ups and shuffle into the dugout as Craig approaches Coach Balfoure, who's hunched over a lineup card.

"Hey Coach, got a minute?" Craig says as he extends a hand to Balfoure for a handshake.

"Yeah, hey, where's Alex? Thinking about starting him in right field today, but I haven't seen him."

"That would have been nice, but that's actually why I'm here," Craig says, breathing deeply. Balfoure, for the first time since Craig can remember, meets his eyes. He pauses for a moment. "Yeah, well, Jennifer and I talked about it, and we've decided to step away from the team. No hard feelings. It just hasn't been a good fit."

"Oh, OK, well thank you for telling me," Balfoure says.

"I just think he needs a break from it all," Craig says, narrowing his eyes, holding tight to the coach's meaty, calloused hand. "We're thinking wrestling for Alex maybe, you know what with his size and all. Let him grapple with those little guys."

"Yeah maybe," Balfoure says, pulling away from the long handshake. "Well, like I said, thanks for letting me know. I've got to get back to it."

"Right." Craig clenches his jaw, fans his hands wide and then balls them into fists, repeating the gesture again and again. He walks quickly to his wife and the other baseball moms gathered next to the aluminum bleachers and huddled around cardboard boxes and an ice chest.

"OK, Jennifer, it's done. You stay here. I'm going to shoot the shit with Patrick and Seth. We might as well take in one more game."

Jennifer tries to gauge her husband's anger, his frustration, and his sobriety. Before she can read his eyes, Craig has turned his back and begun his escape from the baseball moms.

Jennifer turns to her friends. "Well, ladies, some of you probably already know, but Alex is taking a break from the Sluggers. Craig just told coach. I'm going to miss seeing you all every weekend, but lately it just hasn't been much fun for Alex.

"That's not why I'm here this morning though." Jennifer opens the flaps of the cardboard box at her feet. "The tank tops came out pretty nice, I think. Take one for yourselves, and there's a couple dozen more to sell. I figure every little bit helps. Whether we're with the team or not, Monica, you know we'll always be there for you."

Monica grabs Jennifer and hugs her tight. "Thanks so much girl. I can't tell you how much I appreciate it. The shirts really turned out great. I love you. I'm going to miss you out here."

"I love you too."

The women hold each other tight until their backs begin to shake with their sobs.

Craig slouches his arms against the waist-high fence along the left-field foul line alongside Seth and Patrick. "Well, what's done is done. I'm still here for your boys." Seth barely hears him. A lump forms in his throat and his eyes, his thoughts, and all of his attention are trained on his son running out to take his starting position in right field. *It's too bad about Alex*, he thinks. *But Zach has his chance now to prove himself.*

Craig gulps hard, finishing the last of the Jim Beam. "Let's boy." He pushes down a heavy, frothy burp. "I mean, let's go boys."

Patrick puts a hand on his friend's shoulder, "Pace yourself, Craig."

Seth focuses on the field, rather than Craig's state of intoxication. "Yeah, and look who we have umpiring today; it's Knuckle."

Craig snaps to attention. "No shit, Knuckle again? I swear to God, this guy screws us every time."

One by one the Sluggers are sent back to the dugout on strikeouts.

"God damn it, Knuckle! Call it both ways!" Craig yells. "He couldn't have hit that with a ten-foot pole. You son of a bitch!"

Harry calls time-out, rises from his umpire crouch, and walks slowly on stiff knees and ankles to the Sluggers' dugout, motioning Coach Balfoure to him.

"Coach, you've got to get your parents under control. The rules say I can throw them out when it gets to this point, but I don't want to do that."

"I've got about as much control over these assholes as you have over this game, Knuckle," Balfoure says. "That guy riding your ass doesn't even have a son in the game. I don't know what he's doing here."

"Fine, but I've had it," Harry says as he walks back to his station. He sweeps the dirt from home plate with his small pocket brush.

"That should help, fat ass," Craig yells. The back of his throat fills with the morning's breakfast before he swallows it back down. "It helps. I mean it helps to see the plate."

Harry stiffens, jerks up, and shouts in the general direction of the right-field foul line. "That's it, you're out of here," he says, pointing to Craig, then to the parking lot. "Off the premises. Away from the field."

"I think he's talking to you, Craig," Patrick says.

"Ah, fuck him. I'm out of here. I'll see you whenever."

Harry walks back behind home plate. "OK pitcher, let's go. Play ball!"

Harry "Knuckle" Boyd lumbers away from the field and toward the far end of the parking lot. A plodding pace is the best his large frame and tired knees can manage after ninety minutes crouched behind catchers whose much smaller bodies and still-developing hand-eye co-ordination allow pitch after pitch to strike him in the feet, shins, and chest protector. Aside from the physical exhaustion, the derision in the stands, the heckling, and the need to send a father away have taken a toll. He walks head down, avoiding eye contact with anyone. He's relieved to see that his black, faded Honda Civic is far from the pickup trucks and baseball dads.

Harry pops his trunk and pulls out a folding stool. He rests for a moment before shedding his shin guards and chest protector. He throws all of it into the trunk. A short drive later, he's home: a one-bedroom apartment on the ground floor. He passes by a poster of the Three Tenors—Luciano Pavarotti, José Carreras, and Plácido Domingo—hanging in his small entryway. Harry takes a Gatorade from his mostly empty refrigerator, his third sports drink of the day, and chugs.

In the bathroom, he turns his shower to high heat, basking in the rising steam as the water takes its sweet time to warm up. He wraps himself in a towel, heads out to bring a CD player into the bathroom, and turns the volume high. Pavarotti's version of the aria "Nessun dorma" fills not only his bathroom but also his entire apartment and possibly the ones next door.

Eyes closed, Harry puts his forehead inches from the shower head, taking in the aria and daydreaming of an alternate, similar, maybe slightly better life. Pavarotti's voice sends Harry's thoughts to the 1990 FIFA World Cup. But his memories aren't of Italy, where the soccer tournament was played, but of the pizzeria where he watched segments of the games after his shifts ended, and Pavarotti's version of the aria punctuated the broadcast. During those matches, Harry had wondered, *Wouldn't it be better to be a soccer referee than a baseball umpire? Wouldn't the parents be outside of earshot at soccer matches, more sober, less abrasive? Who knows? And what do I know about soccer anyway?*

Harry opens his eyes, shakes all thoughts of soccer from his mind, and finishes the task of washing the sweat and red dirt from his face, fingernails, and between his toes. He'll be late for work, and the hot water won't last much longer.

Pizza and Pipes isn't far from home. Harry walks through the restaurant's wide, heavy, wooden double doors before his hair is dry. Young baseball players still in uniform and their coaches take up most of the pizzeria and are polishing off their post-game meal. Harry looks around and is relieved not to see anyone from the Sluggers.

Harry makes his way toward the kitchen, past a set of towering organ pipes that to his recollection has never been played, when he walks past a group of particularly rowdy boys with the team name "Rockets" emblazoned across their chests. Coach Greg tries in vain to quiet his team when he notices Harry.

"Hey Knuckle, I mean Harry, what's up man?"

"Oh, hey, Greg. How are you? Looks like you guys won today. How'd it go?"

"Not bad, not bad at all. Actually, we won that tournament. Kind of our last hurrah to be honest."

"Oh yeah, how come? I mean, what's going on with the Rockets? You guys aren't breaking up or anything, are you?"

"No, more like reconstituting," Greg says, lowering his voice to a whisper. "A few of my boys, the best ones, wouldn't you know it, are playing up an age group, so we're combining forces with Balfoure and the Sluggers."

"Oh yeah?"

"Yup. I heard you had a rough go of it this afternoon. Sorry about that. Some of those parents just can't keep their mouths shut. And I know Balfoure can be an asshole, but he and I go way back."

"That's OK," Harry shrugs. "Par for the course. Anyway, I gotta get back to work. Good luck."

"Thanks. You know, I've seen you here before, and I'm sorry I didn't say hi earlier. You always seemed busy. This place is packed after baseball tournaments. Bouncing from umpiring to slinging pizzas, you must be wiped."

"Yeah, I'm definitely not here for the pizza," Harry says, tapping his belly. "Or the pipes."

SIXTH INNING

A PING FROM SETH'S CELL PHONE wakes him a half hour before his alarm. He grabs the phone from its charger and opens his email.

> From: Mark Balfoure
> Subject: Umpires
> Sluggers Parents,

> I know we've had a rough go of it lately with bad umpires, but if the chatter and abuse continue, there won't be any more tournaments to play in. The umpires have had enough. They're not signing up for tourneys, and tournaments are being canceled. Simply put: Without umps, we can't play anything that amounts to more than a scrimmage.

> Unfortunately, we had an ugly incident yesterday where a parent of a former player decided

it was acceptable to berate an umpire. The parent was thrown out. Justifiably. And it could have been worse. Thankfully, our umpire hung in there. I'd much rather have a dad ejected than an umpire quit. Why? Because we can play without you, baseball dads, but we'll always need someone to call balls and strikes. It's no surprise that there is a shortage of umpires and referees in all sports.

We have to be better than this. If you want your son to be on the Sluggers, you have to be better than this. The umpire who took the abuse, from what I suspect was an intoxicated dad, is one of the most highly regarded umpires out there. But that's irrelevant. If he was the worst umpire on the planet, it should not matter. It is not acceptable for parents, spectators, or grandparents to direct ANY comments to our umpires under any circumstances.

For the Sluggers, this is a zero-tolerance policy. What does that mean? I will tell you to leave before the umpire has a chance to eject you. So, what can you do instead? I'm glad you asked. Take a long walk. Preferably far away from the field. Make some friends. Take a deep breath. Remind yourself that these boys aren't even teenagers yet. Buy a hot dog or a cheeseburger.

If grandma or grandpa can't keep their mouths shut because they "hilariously" have no filter, help move their chairs so they can watch from the outfield.

—Coach Balfoure

Seth rubs his eyes. *Jesus, Craig really went out with a bang,* he thinks, resting his phone on his chest. Coach must be pretty pissed to be firing off emails this early in the morning. His phone pings again, this time from a Facebook notification, also from Balfoure. This message wasn't meant for the Sluggers parents alone but also intended to reach baseball dads and moms far and wide.

OPEN TRYOUTS FOR DEDICATED TWELVE AND UNDER PLAYERS. MUST BE COMMITTED TO COMPETITIVE BASEBALL AND TRAVELING OUT OF STATE, INCLUDING COOPERSTOWN TRAVEL BALL WORLD SERIES.

Seth immediately stops scrolling through his feed and bolts upright. Too early in the morning to call, he texts Patrick: "An open tryout? Does he really expect our boys to try out after all the practices, all the games? And the monthly fees we've paid?"

A response comes immediately: "Just saw it. Almost

called Balfoure. I don't know what to think. It's no secret we're merging with the Rockets. Maybe he wants to keep things on the up and up. Probably giving him too much credit."

Seth: "He's an ass. See you at the tryout, I guess."

The tryout meets Balfoure's expectations. His new Sluggers team sheds players he's never liked, adds talent from the Rockets, and takes in a few strays who should work out nicely. And hopefully the shake-up keeps the complaining, second-guessing dads in line. This is a team he can take to Cooperstown.

Finally, it's seven in the morning. After hours of watching reruns of home renovation shows, Monica rises from bed having had zero sleep and calls her son's middle school.

"Hi Elise, it's Monica. Just wanted to let you know Zach won't be at school today. Yeah, it's a doctor's appointment, well, my appointment. He's coming with me to my chemo treatment today. Seth can't make it because of work, and Zach's worried about me being alone . . . Yes, he's a sweet boy. Anyway, just wanted to make sure you have him down as an excused absence . . . Thank you, I appreciate it. It's going well. I'll talk to you later."

In a room full of recliners and intravenous drips, Zach stares at the timer on his cell phone. "Three . . . two . . . one. OK, Mom, it's time. Here we go." Zach opens a cooler packed with dry ice and pulls out a cap that vaguely resembles those worn by rugby players. He yanks it onto his mother's head.

"Not so rough, Zach."

"It's got to be on tight, Mom. Hold still. There you go."

Zach resets the timer and checks to make sure the cooler is closed and sealed.

"Thank you, baby, for coming and helping me," Monica says. "You're really good at this. I love you."

"Sure, Mom," he says without looking up from the backward counting seconds on his phone.

Seth climbs into his truck and notes the time, three thirty in the afternoon. Leaving work early means he'll be at the treatment center much earlier than he needs to be.

With the extra time, he stops at the Sluggers' fireworks stand, where the sale of sparklers, smoke balls, and rockets will subsidize the team's trip to Cooperstown. He's relieved to see Coach Greg working the stand and not Balfoure.

"Hey, Coach, thought I'd find you here. Figured I'd stop by and see how things were going," Seth says.

"Good. It's been busy. If we keep pace, we should make about $5,000," Greg says. "It gets hot inside this tinderbox, but you can't beat it as a fundraiser."

"That's great. Cooperstown isn't going to be cheap, but we sure are looking forward to it," Seth says. "Looking forward to Vegas too. I checked out those Big League Dreams fields online, and they look pretty sweet."

"I think the boys will have fun," Greg says. "It's good we're all staying in the same hotel. The boys can swim after games, and we can all hang out by the pool. We'll go to dinners together, all that. I'm hoping the boys get to know each other better at this tournament, you know, really bond. I'd like us to all be a team, a real team, by the time we get to Cooperstown."

"Yeah, like I said, we're excited," Seth says. "Really happy with how Zach's been swinging the bat lately. Looking forward to watching him on those fields. You know, I tell him all the time, there are about three hundred Division 1 baseball programs, and just as many in Division 2 and 3. That's nearly a thousand college teams, and only one has to take a chance on him. Anyway, see you at practice."

Greg shakes his head as Seth returns to his truck.

It's the first Saturday morning of the summer when Craig isn't checking his son's baseball bag to make sure it's packed with his mitt, batting gloves, cleats, and bat. He's not rousing Alex from his bed and gathering his uniform and rushing to make sure he has enough break-fast in his belly to fuel him for two games.

A weekend without baseball, and Craig is at ease. He figures warm-ups are about to begin for the Slug-gers' first game in Las Vegas, but the fear of missing out that he anticipated would hang over this Saturday and Sunday is absent. The urge to text Seth and Patrick for game updates never materializes. He finishes the last forkful of his scrambled eggs and the final bite of bacon. Tossing his plastic plate in the sink, he walks to Alex's room.

His son is still deep asleep, tangled in a sheet and blanket, his bare legs exposed, and his head buried in pillows. Craig runs his fingers through his son's messy hair and kisses the back of his head.

It's nine in the morning, the house is quiet, and Craig has nowhere to be. He returns to the kitchen to clean a frying pan, plate, and fork. He tidies up the living room and scans the house for anything else that can be done. Seeing no outstanding chores, Craig grabs a leash from a hook next to his front door and, to his dog Rowdy's delight, heads into the neighborhood for an hour-long walk.

When he returns, Craigs checks on Alex again to find his son still in a slumber. He sighs, bored and a little lonely, and strides to his backyard shed for the lawn mower. In thirty minutes, the grass is cut and, more importantly, the noise was enough to wake Alex who is shoveling cereal into his mouth when Craig walks into the kitchen for water.

"Why don't we play some Wiffle ball out front when you're done with breakfast?" Craig asks. Alex shrugs.

"Well think about it, but after breakfast you need to at least change out of your pajamas. You have to get outside at some point today and before it gets too hot. I'll tell you what, I have some more yard work to do out front. Once you're dressed, meet me out there, and I'll throw you some pitches."

"Fine," Alex mumbles through a mouthful of Rice Krispies.

Craig tries to hide his surprise when fifteen minutes later Alex appears in the driveway with a yellow plastic bat in one hand and two white plastic balls in the other. Craig tosses his pruning shears to the middle of the lawn and hustles to the front of the driveway.

"Here, toss me the balls. You remember the rules: Hard ground balls are singles; line drives into the street doubles; balls to the opposite sidewalk triples; and anything beyond that, well, you know, home run."

"I know the game, Dad. Just throw strikes."

Craig bounces his first pitch a foot in front of Alex. His next pitch sails behind his son's head and bangs off the garage door. Alex drops his bat and steps toward the front door without saying a word. "Shit," Craig says, grabbing the yellow bat as it rolls down the driveway. "Wait a second, wait a second. Just give me a chance to warm up. It's been a while. I'll find the strike zone."

Alex moves his gaze from the pavement to his dad and turns just enough to grab the bat. With zero enthusiasm, he takes a lackadaisical batting stance. Craig fires a waist-high pitch. "Strike one. I told you. Now let's go!"

Craig's next pitch is nearly as perfect, and Alex shoots a line drive into the street. "Nice!" Craig says as he jogs to retrieve the ball.

Father and son fall into a rhythm of pitches delivered down the middle of an imaginary plate and hits that are smacked at twice the speed into the street, to the opposite sidewalk. Finally, Alex sends a white plastic ball into the front yard across the street. "Say goodbye, Dad. That ball is gone!" Alex shouts, tossing his bat before trotting around pretend bases.

In Las Vegas, Seth settles into his stadium-style seat complete with a cupholder for his twenty-ounce souvenir cup filled with Coors Light. The Big League Dreams field surpasses his expectations with its perfect artificial turf infield, natural grass outfield, and towering wooden fence painted to replicate Dodger Stadium. He allows himself to have his own big league daydream in which he is a spectator as his son takes the field for his first professional game. As Zach basks in the glow of a sports cathedral, the young man's eyes will lock on his father's, and in that moment all the little league games, travel ball tournaments, and pep talks will wash over Seth. The moment, he imagines, will be more beautiful than seeing his life flash through his consciousness before he passes into the great beyond.

The Sluggers start to take the field, and Seth pops out of his reverie to scan the outfield for Zach but finds him still in the dugout. Gulping hard on his beer, he feels Monica's hand take his. Seth slumps in his seat and watches the game unfold, his daydream vanishing with each inning Zach sits on the dugout bench.

When Zach finally takes an outfield position, his focus switches to the infield; a drama unfolds between pitcher, catcher, and coach. Pitch after pitch bounces off Rick's catcher's gear as Jason struggles to throw anything close to the strike zone. Balfoure shifts on his bucket positioned outside the dugout, squirming like a man with a recurring hemorrhoid. He spits and quietly admonishes himself for trusting that Jason, with the help from his private pitching coach, would finally own the strike zone. Balfoure's words for his pitcher can be heard throughout the stands and sound more of admonishment than advice. Rick trots to the pitcher's mound, and, while the conversation is inaudible to the parents in the stands, the catcher's wild gestures and the final slam of the ball into Jason's glove make it clear the catcher/coach's son and coach/father are equally disgusted.

Jason smiles nervously. His right arm tingles, and sweat from his right palm makes the ball feel moist and a little slick. His next pitch bounces two feet in front of the plate and hits the thumb on Rick's throwing hand. Rick lurches forward from his catcher's squat and drops face-mask-first into the dirt. Balfoure rises from his bucket, but before he can walk to his son, Greg calls time-out and paces toward home plate.

"You OK, Rick?" Greg says, pulling him up by his shoulders and then taking his hand to assess the damage. "Let me see you flex your hand, like this."

"I'm fine. Why is he out there smiling while we're getting killed?"

"Alright, looks like you're OK. You're a tough kid, but listen: Everybody shows their nerves in different ways. He's trying his hardest. Maybe trying too hard. Your job as a catcher is to calm him down, help him out, get the best out of him. Now you sure you're OK?"

Rick nods.

"Then let's get this last out, get back in the dugout, and get these runs back."

Greg jogs back to the dugout, and Balfoure extends his arm for a handshake, quickly pulls it away and slaps him hard on the ass. "That was quite a pep talk. Let's see if it does any good."

The next pitch is hit on a line toward Zach. He barely moves, doesn't have to move, and the ball pops into the webbing of his glove. Third out. Inning over. "At least Jason finally threw a strike," Balfoure mumbles in Greg's direction. "We got lucky." Greg pretends not to hear, hustles toward the field and high-fives the boys as they come off the diamond.

The Sluggers get some of the runs back, but not all, and after the game, Balfoure turns to one of his often-tried, rarely true motivational tactics. After a lengthy post-game speech in which Balfoure reminds them of their errors, strikeouts, and other miscues, he instructs them to change out of their cleats and put on their sneakers.

"You boys owe me some wind sprints," he says before leading them to an empty portion of the stadium's parking lot.

"Coach Balfoure," Greg says, "What do you say we just call it a day? Everyone just wants to get back to the hotel."

Balfoure stares ahead. His pace quickens toward the back of the expansive parking lot. The new members of the team, most of whom played for Greg's Rockets, are bewildered but take their cues from the veteran Sluggers. The boys form a line and look up at Balfoure's raised hand. When he quickly lowers it, they sprint until Balfoure instructs them to stop; they turn around and look to him again. They repeat the routine until Greg interrupts.

"That's enough," he says. "Boys, I'll see you back at the hotel. Make sure you've got all your gear."

Balfoure heads straight to his truck, ignores the parents' stares and scowls, loads up Rick's catcher's gear, and speeds away. Greg's gaze remains fixed on Balfoure's tailgate until it's out of sight. His eyes then turn to twelve tired players and two dozen parents, who are equal parts exasperated and enraged.

"I'm going to order some pizza, have it delivered to the hotel pool deck," Greg says. "Let's head back, get changed, and I'll meet you all there."

It's not long before cannon balls and games of keep-away and Marco Polo wash away the boys' disappointment. Not so for the parents. They eat pepperoni pizza and sip cocktails in silence, looking at one another, hoping someone will break the silence and say what they're all thinking.

Finally, from a parent of the Rockets ex-pats: "Greg, this is not what we signed up for. I think I speak for all of us when I say that I'm tired of Balfoure's lectures, the negativity, his abrasiveness. Just everything that comes out of his mouth. We came over to this team because of you, but quite frankly, it's not worth it if this is what we have to look forward to. And I'm speaking only for myself here, but I'm not going to fly cross-country just to have this asshole berate my kid for a week. Cooperstown or not, it's not the experience we're looking for. Far from it."

The parents nod in unison.

"I don't like it either," Greg says. "I've known Mark for a long time, and I know he can be a little rough around the edges, but I didn't know he'd gotten this bad. But I agree with you. Before you decide anything though, let me talk to him. Like I said, we go way back."

Balfoure places the remains of his room service cheese-burger outside his door and lies on the bed next to Rick to watch the last innings of a Dodgers game. He hears a knock and hopes it's not a parent wanting to bitch about today or to beg that their son gets more playing time tomorrow.

He's relieved to see Greg.

"Hey, come on in. You want a beer? Rick and I have the game on."

"Um, no thanks. Actually, can I talk to you in the hallway?"

"Yeah, sure," Mark says, changing his mind and

wishing it was a parent he could easily dispatch. "What's up?"

"I wanted to talk about today. Sometimes, Mark, I think you forget that these are twelve-year-olds. They're going to make mistakes. This isn't like back in junior college. Most of these boys can't handle the kind of ass-chewings we got in JC. At best, it makes them play tight. And I know some of my boys are downright scared of you."

"Scared of me? Looks to me like some of them are scared of the ball."

"Well, I can tell you that it's just not working, and it's not working for a lot of people," Greg says. "I just had a talk with a bunch of the parents, and they're not going to continue if it keeps up. I'm just asking you to take it down a notch."

"This is bullshit," Balfoure says. "You remember when we played for Coach Smith? He ran us until we yacked; he motherfucked us the whole time. And you know what? We're better for it. Our sophomore year, we won a conference title. He was always there for us, you remember that, right? It didn't matter if we were having problems with a professor, or grades, anything."

"I know Mark, but like I said, this isn't junior college. These are boys. You're going to lose this team if you don't lighten up. And if you're really set on going to Cooperstown, you're going to have to make this work. There's just not enough time to put another team together."

"What are you saying? You want to take over? Am I just supposed to sit on my hands and pretend I'm not seeing what I'm seeing? The called third strikes. The boneheaded baserunning, the . . ."

"That's not what I'm saying. I'm saying you need to lighten up a little. Teach them. Talk to them."

"Fuck this. You know what? Go ahead, do it your way. You want to coddle them? Fine. But you won't be doing them any favors. What's going to happen when they get to the next level and are coached hard?"

"Mark, we're talking in circles now. I'm just trying to level with you."

"I've had enough of this bullshit. All of it. It's your team if you want it. You want to buy out my Cooperstown bid, fine, you have until Monday. But I've had enough," Balfoure slams the hotel door. "Rick, pack up your stuff. We're going home."

SEVENTH INNING

MONICA LEANS OVER HER BATHROOM VANITY to study her thinning black hair in the mirror. She plants her hands on the vanity tile and inspects the black and gray strands, fighting the temptation to touch and test their resiliency. *Will they stay? Or fall like so many others?*

Monica delicately runs a hand over the skin just above her left breast, feeling the outline of a small disc-shaped port and a thin tube that connects the port to a large vein. She prays silently that the drugs being pumped into her body will kill the cancer. All of it. *In the name of the father, son, and . . .*

"Hi Zach, how are you baby?"

"Hey Mom, how are *you*? You look pretty." Zach pushes in around the bathroom door. "Here, I brought you a Gatorade and a Popsicle."

"Well, thank you. You keep the Gatorade, but I'll take that Popsicle," she says. "What's up? Are you

71

coming to check on me?"

"No, well yeah, but also to talk. I've been thinking about it, and I'm not so sure I want to go to Cooperstown."

"Why not, baby? I heard you boys played so well in the Las Vegas tournament. And Dad said you got two hits in the championship game. Why wouldn't you want to go?"

Zach looks down at his mismatched socks, trying to unscramble the words bouncing through his mind that he had ordered perfectly moments before walking into the bathroom. "I don't know. I just don't feel like it."

"Zach, come on. What's wrong? I heard Coach Greg is great. It sounds like so much fun. Why wouldn't you want to go?"

"I don't know, maybe Las Vegas would be a good one to end on, at least for this season. And, and," he picks at some paint on the bathroom door, "I don't think Dad and I should be gone for a whole week. I'd rather hang out with you. And who will help with your cold caps? You know I'm the best."

"Zach, I don't want you to miss out because of me. Jaclyn will go with me to chemo, and she may not be the best like you, but she'll be great," Monica says, forcing a slight smile she hopes will reassure her son.

"Mom, I'm not going! I'm staying here with you!" He feels tears begin to well in his eyes and retreats to his room.

Monica and Seth talk late into the night. For the first time since her diagnosis, they discuss their fears that the disease might not go away, may spread, or return even if the chemo is successful. And they talk about their son in ways they never have before. Not about his grades. Not about his play on the baseball field. They talk about the ways he looks after shy children on the playground and in the dugout. Mostly they talk about the outsized support he's lent Monica; his refusal to leave her side. They are proud, and they are heartbroken. They've never forced him to play, and they're not about to start now.

After explaining Zach's decision to Greg the following day, Seth points out the obvious: the open spot on the Sluggers' twelve-player roster. He suggests Greg bring back one of the Sluggers' original members: Alex.

Alex hadn't quit because he stopped loving the game or the team, Seth assures him. In fact, his teammates were the closest thing he had to friends. He hadn't really quit at all. Craig quit for his son, fed up with Coach Balfoure's abrasiveness and fear that Alex would recoil from the game. Now with Balfoure gone . . .

"I'd be fine with it, but there's just one problem. Big problem," Greg says. "Every team has to bring an umpire with them to Cooperstown. And we've been talking to Harry Boyd."

Craig pulls open the heavy wooden doors of Pizza and Pipes and steps in slowly, seeing nothing until his eyes eventually adjust to the darkness of the cavernous restaurant. He scans the dining room for the manager and spots him helping a teenage girl working the register.

"Knuck—I mean Harry, you got a sec?"

Harry vaguely recognizes the man. His voice sounds familiar, but something in the man's tone is off.

"Sure. Take a seat in the back, and I'll get us some waters."

Craig is rolling a napkin in the palms of his sweaty hands when Harry returns and squeezes into an overstuffed vinyl booth across from him.

"Well, what's up then?"

"I heard you're going with Greg's team to Cooperstown. That you're their sponsored umpire. Congrats, that's great. You've been umping for a long time, right?"

Harry nods. He recognizes the man across from him

now. "You're missing a great game, Knuckle!" Harry glances at the teenager at the register and watches her tentatively tap the buttons; he wishes this man with his contrived reconciliatory tone would get to the point.

Craig tries again. "Ever been to Cooperstown before?"

"I started umpiring when I was still in high school. Have done it off and on ever since. Long enough to see kids I umped in under-eights come into this place as teens, college kids. Yeah, long time. And nope, never been," Harry says, looking over Craig closely now, watching as bits of napkin fall from his hand. If this fidgety, sweaty man won't get to the point, he will.

"It took me a minute to place you, but I know now. I heard we picked up a new family for Cooperstown."

"Yeah, that's actually why I'm here."

"No kidding? It's not for the two-slice lunch special?"

"Ha, ha. No, I stopped by because, because I wanted to apologize for giving you such a hard time in the past. I don't know why I get so worked up. I know the booze doesn't help—and Greg made me promise to stay sober at the games—hell, I don't know why I even care so much about the games. I guess I just want good things for Alex. I don't know how much you know about

Alex, but baseball, his teammates . . . if not for that, he wouldn't have much."

"There's nothing wrong with that, caring and wanting the best for Alex, but you have to understand something. Umpires are going to miss calls. Call a ball a strike. A fair ball foul. And the boys, they're going to space out on the basepaths, turn into boneheaded base runners for no apparent reason. Drop pop-ups. But it's not because we don't care. It's not because we don't want to catch it or make every call. Jesus, look at you, look how bad you want it, and you're not even out there on the field."

"I know. No shit. I get all that. But what I don't get, Harry, is why you do it. And for all these years, why you're still calling games? Taking all the abuse?"

"There's just something about it. Flawed people in a perfect game," Harry says, "Nobody out there is going to grow up to be Ted Williams or Sandy Koufax. And despite what you parents think, your boys aren't going to play past high school or even past youth league. Most of us, we're lucky to experience the game and everything about it for just the blink of an eye. I like to think that in my way I give the boys a shot at that. Even if they spend the better part of a weekend swinging and missing, the one time they barrel up a ball, it's worth it. It's perfect."

"Jesus Knuckle . . . Harry, you may not always ump a good game, but you sure can talk one," Craig says, smiling for the first time. "Listen, I appreciate you hearing me out, and I'm looking forward to hanging out once we get there. You'll have to let me buy you a beer."

Harry is happy to not have an opportunity to share beers with Craig or any of the parents. The umpires share a large rental house in Cooperstown. Groups of parents split their own rental homes. Nobody is more pleased with the housing arrangements than the players. The boys stay in dormitories, cram into musty bedrooms, and share bunk beds. The only time their parents see them is when they're on the field. And even then, they barely hear from them.

The experience is both odd and wonderful. The voices of their teammates, their coaches, and umpires are louder than their parents. No one pokes at their backs through the chain-link fence of the dugout.

They glance into the stands every now and then, find their parents in the crowd. But for the seven games they'll play in Cooperstown, they're immersed in the baseball, nothing but baseball. They lean against a padded railing that separates the dugout from the field. Yell, "Ooooooh, I like that!" when a teammate swings hard—as hard as he can, harder than his dad would say he should—and misses. Because the miss doesn't matter, not here, not when there will be no post-game evaluation of every at bat.

After each game, players return to their dorms. Still laughing. Bragging about base hits, a diving play, near misses. "I was just under it, but I was on it." They strip off their grass-stained uniforms and socks filled with crushed red clay, stuff them into bags that will be taken to be washed for the next game. Then it's video games, jeering, and cheering. Teammates and players from states they've never been to, from states they couldn't identify on a map; they all watch major league games together on TV. They argue about which of the players on screen are trash, who's the man, who is going to carry their fantasy baseball team to a win. The bedrooms and the common areas all smell like an armpit the size of a baseball diamond. Only the volunteers and tournament officials notice.

At the rental homes, dads discover they have more in common than their quest for discounted bats and YouTube instructional videos. Their time away from the fields is still occupied with booze and barbecue grills, but less with talk of baseball. They chatter about shitty bosses. Plan summer camping trips. At the end of the night, they can't recall the score of the game they watched hours earlier.

Days pass like this. The Sluggers won't play more than their seven guaranteed games. Won't make the championship round or even a consolation game. The team has won two of its six games so far. Or was it three of six? The players, the parents, no one is quite sure. But tomorrow will be the last game.

Alex tucks in his uniform and breathes deeply. *God, I hope today is the day. It's got to be. Dear God,* he thinks, *please let today be the day.* He's the only Slugger without a hit in this tournament. Couple of walks, he reached base when that huge kid hit him. Couple of weak ground balls that he knew were destined to be outs; so much so that it was barely worth the effort to run to first base. But not one hit. The math is easy; he has a .000 batting average for the tournament.

God, let today be the day.

The Sluggers are down four runs in the seventh inning. For twelve-year-olds, games finish at the end of the seventh, and the Sluggers' tournament is nearing its conclusion. However, the inevitability of another loss is only apparent on the scoreboard. As the Sluggers take their last at bats, players line the dugout railing— smiling, spitting sunflower seeds, and cheering each pitch with the joy of a team on the precipice of a World Series victory but with none of the anxiety.

Alex, however, is far from carefree. Down to his final strike and the brink of striking out in his third and final at bat of the game, Alex strangles the handle of his bat. Harry, umpiring this final game, also feels pangs of anxiety. *Swing the bat, kid. Please swing the bat. Don't make me be the one to call a third strike with the bat still on your shoulder.*

Alex swings, and a strange vibration radiates from his hands to his elbows and through to his shoulders. He races down the first base line. Head down, white chalk races quickly beneath him. Very soon he expects to hear the slap of a ball against leather. He looks up to avoid crashing into the first baseman, sure to be stretching for the ball and sealing his .000 tournament batting average. To his astonishment, first base is unoccupied. In his peripheral vision, he sees that the first baseman is several feet from the bag. Alex lunges at first base, and his momentum carries him several more feet down the line. Turning toward the infield, he sees the shortstop casually receiving a relay throw from the outfield.

Sounds of jubilation from the Sluggers' dugout rush into Alex's head. He hears his name shouted in high-pitched screams. He hears it too from the stands, incomprehensible shrills from moms and deep-throated yells from dads.

Alex trots a few steps back to the bag. *Don't smile*, he thinks, *don't smile*. He toes first base and looks across the field at his teammates, still pounding the railing and squealing. He'd wanted to wink or pound his chest, pump his fists or point, but all he can manage is a deep exhale.

Three thousand miles away, Balfoure stares at his cell phone, satisfied that the Sluggers will return home a beaten team. With the help of a live-game app, he watches as their final outs tick down. In digital form, a dot with Alex's name moves from the batter's box to first base. Single. Balfoure clicks off his phone, tosses it aside, and crushes his last Coors Light of the day.

As their plane takes off to carry the Sluggers home, the cabin is filled with a bouncing energy and cacophony matched only by their flight from Los Angeles to Las Vegas. By the time the 747 reaches its cruising altitude, the boys have either found sleep or a movie.

Harry walks down the aisle until he finds Alex slouched against Craig, squirming for a comfortable position in which he can nap. Harry taps Alex on the shoulder and crouches to eye level with the boy. The old umpire hands him a baseball and whispers just loud enough for both father and son to hear:

"That was perfect."

About the Author

MATT LEEDY is a former reporter for newspapers including *The Express-Times, The Sun,* and *The Fresno Bee.* He lives in California with his wife, daughter, son, and two dogs. This is his first novella.